D1256356

www.mascotbooks.com

The Story of the Can't That Could

For more information, please contact:
Mascot Books
620 Herndon Parkway, Suite 320
Herndon, VA 20170
info@mascotbooks.com

Library of Congress Control Number: 2019901393

CPSIA Code: PRT0419A
ISBN-13: 978-1-64307-245-6

Printed in the United States

The Story of the
CAN'T
That
COULD

Joan C. Yingling

Illustrated by Ana Sebastian

Now, I'm sure you've heard of the Three Little Bears

And about the race
of the Tortoise and Hare,

Of the walk that was taken
by Red Riding Hood,

But have you ever heard of
THE CAN'T THAT COULD?

Can't was sitting on a rock one day,
Watching the Coulds having fun at play.

How they laughed and had such fun,
But Can't just sat, wishing he was one.

He started to cry, feeling sorry for himself

When he heard the voice of a wee little elf.

"OH NO, I CAN'T DO ANYTHING RIGHT. I SIT AND CRY ALL DAY AND ALL NIGHT."

"WELL, THAT'S THE TROUBLE,"

said the elf.

"YOU WASTE TIME FEELING SORRY FOR YOURSELF."

"IF YOU FOREVER JUST SIT AND CRY,
ALWAYS WISHING, BUT NEVER TRY,

The little elf turned and went on his way

And Can't started thinking about what the elf had to say.

The next day,
can't did something new,

Surprising himself with the things he could do.

And the secret was, he had to say,
A little verse that went this way.

"COULD NOT CAN'T
IS WHAT I'LL SAY.
TRY IS WHAT
I'LL DO EACH DAY.

CAN'T IS ONLY FOR THE LAZY ONE,
COULD CAN ALWAYS GET
SOMETHING DONE.

The END

ABOUT THE AUTHOR

Joan C. Yingling (1930 – 2008)

My mother, Joan, began writing at a young age. The earliest writing we know of was a poem about her younger brother's first step. Throughout her life, she wrote many stories in verse but only a few were saved in a manila folder for the past five decades.

Recently, I pulled that folder out and marveled once again at my mother's talent. Her stories are so creative and imaginative that I felt compelled to share them with readers everywhere.

The Story of the Can't that Could is the first in a series I hope to share with you. As a mother of seven children, I'm sure Joan heard the words "I can't" a lot. This story has always been a family favorite, and I hope it will become one of yours as well.

Joan passed away on Valentine's Day in 2008. Her beloved husband, Edwin, who is now 92 years old, misses her terribly and wishes she were still here to see the characters of her stories come to life.

-Lydia Cohn, 2019